5 LITTLE WARDENS

Bibs's Room

MAHDIS KIA

To order additional copies of this book, contact:
Xlibris
1-888-795-4274
www.Xlibris.com
Orders@Xlibris.com

ISBN: Softcover   978-1-9845-7908-9
         EBook   978-1-9845-7907-2

Print information available on the last page

Rev. date: 05/27/2020

"5 Little Wardens" is about five tiny seahorses, with giant characters who live in the bottom of the ocean and despite of their core differences they can manage to remain positive and solve all the issues thrown at them in every day ocean-life. With the attitude of being the guardians of the whole ocean, these 5 Little Wardens, attempt to big job which in this series of 'Bibs's Room', involves supporting their friend to keep his room clean and tidy in a reaction towards how the clutter has occurred in first place.

There are couple reasons why there is 5 characters in this book:

Each seahorse represents one element of nature 'Earth', 'Air', 'Fire', 'Water', and 'Spiritual force' or 'Space' just like the five rings of Olympics demonstrating all of us a whole. Also each of these beautiful creatures have different sexual orientations of 'Masculine', 'Feminine', 'Femininity in Men', 'Masculinity in Women' and 'Neutral'. In attempts to better comprehend human sexual complexities, Klein Sexual Orientation Grid (KSOG) was introduced by (Klein, 1978), to detect where people may fit on the HYPERLINK "https://en.wikipedia.org/wiki/Sexual_orientation"sexual spectrum, but to this day individuals, families and friends struggle to cope and act appropriately at the moment of necessity. This is why I trust it's decent to have a fresh practice towards different sexual orientations from early ages of education.

Each of five books from "5 Little Wardens" series addresses a different issue, 'Bibs's Room' tends to highlight our responsibilities in providing an immaculate environment for beautiful creatures of the nature.

With special thanks to my family and friends who have always been great inspiration.

This book is dedicated to the children of the world, namely my beautiful angels: Dorsa, Nickie, Rusty, Hannah, Roddin, Parmys, Rohan, and my cute niece Rosha.

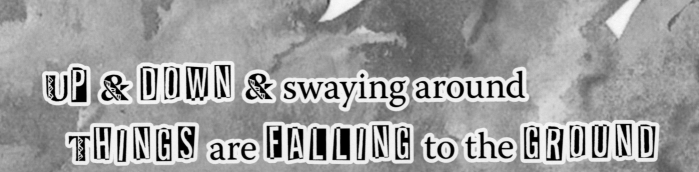

UP & DOWN & swaying around
THINGS are FALLING to the GROUND

Oopsie!

Bubbles!

Bang it crumbles!

Blimp & Blump & Blimp & Blump
Tell my friends about the BUMP

Heads up
    & Hear me out
A thing's fallen like a clout

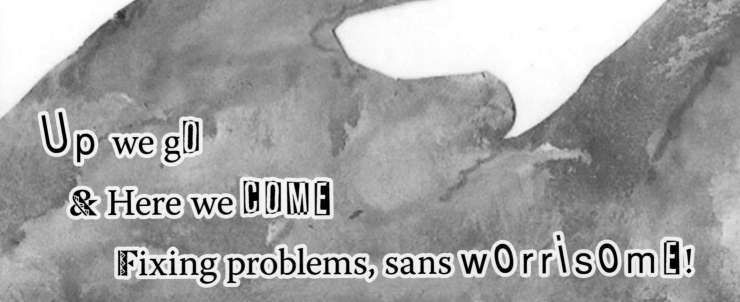

Up we g0
& Here we COME
Fixing problems, sans w0rr\s0mE!

Keeping CalM,
Sweeping the Room,
Each of them had their
own BrOOm.

Singing SONGS
AND Making JOKES
Hoping NOTHING tOssEd by Folks

Bibs was feeling really Blessed
Promised to keep his Room at Best.

We're the **WARDENS** 5 of us!
We keep the **OCEAN** like our **HOUSE**.

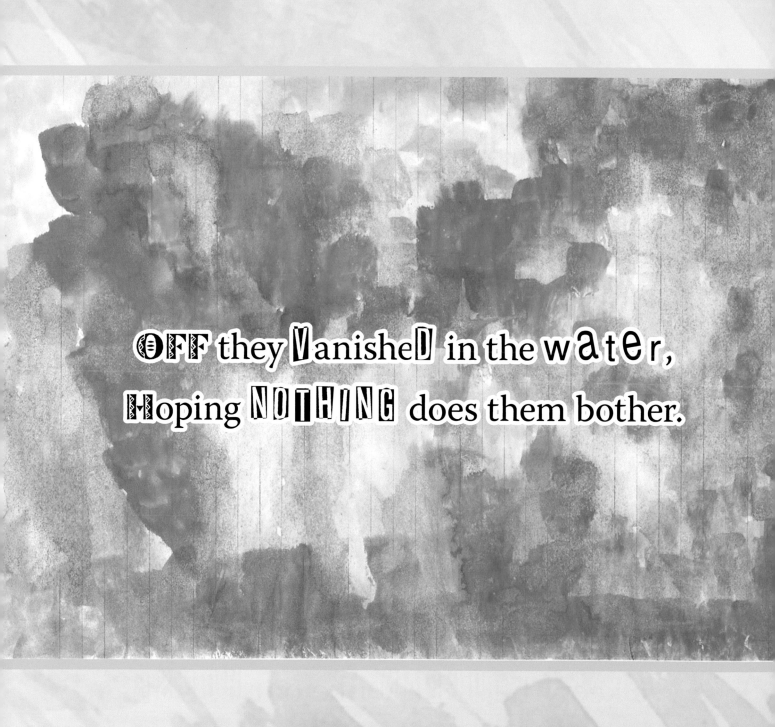

Off they Vanished in the water,
Hoping NOTHING does them bother.

THE END

About The Author

Mahdis Kia was born in 1984 in Tehran, she lived most of her life in Iran. Traveling the world with her family created a collection of memories of diverse cultures, enabling her to think beyond borders and customs. Mahdis accomplished her Masters in Business Administration in 2014 and graduated with a degree in Industrial Management in 2007, spending years in the corporate world since. She moved to beautiful Brisbane on 2017 and finds solace on the coastline and in the forests of the sub tropics.

Art in any shape, interior design and protecting our natural environment have always been absolute passions all along her professional career, adding love, meaning and value to her life.

The current unprecedented events of living in ISO due to the global pandemic and exposure of COVID-19, provided the time and solitude to create a series of 5 children's books following the adventures of 5 delightful and colorful seahorses, serving the purpose of educational entertainment nurturing a love of the natural environment in children.

With special thanks to my family and friends who have always been great inspiration.

This book is dedicated to the children of the world, namely my beautiful angels:

Dorsa, Nickie, Rusty, Hannah, Roddin, Parmys, Rohan, and my cute niece Rosha.

I hope everyone falls in love with Bibs, Salvy, Starsh, Bow, Joyas as much as I have.

Printed in the United States
By Bookmasters